ERNIE A. LEE

Nerdluck on Wheels

Humorous Adventures of a Teenage Driver

Contents

III   In the Army

Acknowledgement

I would like to express my sincere gratitude to my boyfriend, Kevin, for his patience and encouragement while I worked on this project. I would also like to thank him for his advice and assistance with research when I got stuck.

I also want to thank my publisher, Erin.

Dedication

This book is dedicated to my dad, Willee, for his always present support, encouragement, and understanding. He told these with a grin - please read it with one. You might be able to laugh at nobody getting hurt.

I

That Old Gray Chevy Ain't What She Used to Be

'Tis a set of stories about the gray '50 Chevy.

Acquiring the Car

Willee, der Nerd as he would call himself later in life, was taught to drive by his uncle in a 1959 Chevy. It was a four-door hardtop with a two-barrel 283 CID engine. It was Saint Louis, Missouri in 1962, a couple of months before Willee would turn sixteen. Driving practice went well overall. There were no major incidents despite Uncle Gene being constantly afraid the kid would knock out some mailboxes since he always hung too close to the right side of the road.

Willee's father, Lenny, worked at a Chevy dealership. He was a tie-wearing Business Manager, BM for short. He had a company car that Willee was not allowed to drive because of the insurance. In order to drive anything, he would have to buy it. He was ready to get moving but his father wouldn't let him buy a car until Gene decided Willee had enough experience with the basics. Lenny put this restriction on because he was worried about what car his son would choose.

Immediately after Gene offered to teach Willee to drive, Lenny started watching the dealership for good deals. He was looking forward to having a second driver around the house and quickly found a good starter car that could last a while.

The dealership had a couple of big trucks that got sold to a dealership in Washington State. Two guys had driven down to get them and had used a 1949 Chevy four-door to get down to Saint Louis. It only used two quarts of oil during the entire two thousand mile trip. It was then on the wholesale lot for forty dollars.

Lenny was eager to tell his son about it. Before he had a chance to talk to him, Willee had a couple of opportunities to see what was at the dealership. He did not want a four-door car. One that did appeal to him was the one-owner gray car with less than seventy thousand miles selling for a hundred twenty-five dollars.

Lenny argued. He didn't think it was a good idea to pay more than triple the price just to have something that looks cooler. He really tried to convince his son. His brother-in-law, Uncle Gene, stepped in and took Willee's side. In the end, it was Willee's money. Lenny chose to bite his tongue and accept it. His son will make mistakes.

Soda Bottle Barbershop

The cops stopped Willee on Brown Road just after ten at night. He pulled into a barbershop a little south of the Rock Road when he heard the siren. He'd had his car less than a month but needed money for gas. He was with some friends from high school driving around an alley gathering discarded soda bottles behind businesses that were closed for the day. They wanted to get deposits back on the soda bottles at two cents each to buy gas which was seventeen cents per gallon.

The cops stood all four of them up in front of a barbershop, shining their car's spotlight on the group while asking what they had been doing in the alley. There were a few tools and spare parts in the trunk of that 1950 Chevy along with a couple dozen soda bottles. The cops wanted to make sure the tools and parts weren't stolen.

Willee, standing against the wall tense with dread, hoped the cops wouldn't notice the lawn mowing money paper clipped to the sun visor. If they found that, all four teens might end up in jail.

He was so anxious that he hadn't even noticed one of the guy's parents drive by. They saw their son in the spotlight but they kept going. They were too embarrassed to stop and ask the cops what he'd gotten in trouble for. He got in trouble with them later.

After talking to each of the four, the cops believed they were just picking up discarded soda bottles and let them go. Willee restrained himself from burning rubber as he was leaving the barbershop parking lot.

"Willee, mow lawns with me. You'll get more money than with these old soda bottles," said Rich. "I'll need a ride anyway."

Willee thought about that. He hated mowing his own lawn but he rarely had to. His dad wanted to do it himself most of the time so it would be done right. It was only his job when his dad was desperate. "I guess I could do that. I'll see if I can use my dad's trimmer, too."

A Break from Brakes

Willee and a friend were near Alton Dragway. They were leaving after watching some races when they noticed a problem with the car.

Willee saw the tell-tale fluid on the wall of the right rear tire. He knew enough about cars to be sure it was brake fluid from the wheel cylinder. "I've never replaced a wheel cylinder. Let's see if one of the mechanics can help," Willee said to his friend.

They walked around a bit until they found a pit crew putting their dragster on the trailer. Willee and his friend asked if the crew could help with the brakes.

"No, we don't know anything about stopping, only about going faster."

The crew did, however, give Willee a can of brake fluid to get the guys home okay.

Willee, der Nerd, had been reading sports car magazines for several years and knew that Formula One drivers could finish races with no brakes. He was determined that brake failure would never be a traumatic experience.

This was only the beginning of nerdluck on wheels.

The Mailbox

One weekend Willee decided to visit a friend, Jimmy, who had moved fifteen miles west.

He'd gotten there okay even though the brakes on that old gray Chevy were still not working and there was no more brake fluid to add. He learned to double-clutch and downshift into low, then shut off the ignition to make the car stop.

Upon leaving, Willee put the car in reverse and ran down the streetside mailbox.

Double-clutching doesn't help when going from reverse to first. He ground it into first and smoked the clutch to bring that car to a halt before hitting anything else.

Jimmy and his parents ran outside to see what happened while Willee got out of the car to check the damage. The mailbox wasn't completely destroyed but would definitely need to be replaced. Willee worked out a deal with Jimmy's parents that he'd be back the following weekend to do that.

After his embarrassment, he headed home with no better brakes than he arrived with.

The only problem he encountered was a black 1940 Dodge panel truck that decided to stop on Page for a *yellow* light. Willee had to use his emergency brake to keep down with the Dodge truck. Willee was prepared to stop for red but not for *yellow*.

Although, having no brakes, it is probably wrong to say der Nerd was prepared to stop at all.

On Monday at school, he was talking to a friend named Benny.

"Can you give me a ride to the gas station after school?" Benny's father managed several FINA gas stations and Willee would sometimes drive Benny to one of them where he would be a pump jockey for the evening.

On the way to the gas station, Willee told Benny about hitting the mailbox.

"Are you gonna replace the wheel cylinder then?"

"I'll think about it but I'm getting better with practice."

"I don't want to crash someday when I'm just trying to get to work."

That evening at dinner, Willee brought up the idea of getting the wheel cylinder replaced. They'd worked it out that on Tuesday after school he would drop the car off at the dealership and his dad would drive him home.

The following weekend, he showed up to replace the mailbox, which went without a hitch. He shot the breeze with Jimmy and a couple of his teenage neighbor friends for a few minutes before heading home to relax. He would later be grateful for the practice he'd gotten at driving without brakes. For now, he was disappointed it had come to an end. He'd watch for his next opportunity to practice that crucial skill.

Go-Cart Racing

On a warm day in June 1962, Willee went for a ride in that old Chevy at about nine in the morning. As he was passing a local park he heard an engine revving and went to check it out. There he saw Mike, a friend from grade school. Mike had been going around the parking lot with his go-cart but had since pulled it under a shade tree at the back of his parents' house, which bordered the park, and was turning the engine.

Der Nerd cruised up to Mike. "Hey, wanna race? My car against your go-cart."

"You can't turn corners fast enough in that old stove bolt."

"Can too."

"Okay, I'll race but you're gonna lose."

Mike started the go-cart engine and pulled even with the front bumper of that gray Chevy. Mike's younger brother did the countdown and they took off around the parking lot. The Chevy burned rubber but Mike got around the first turn faster. The gray car did *not* corner as well as the go-cart. But Mike was not outdistancing der Nerd by much. Mike felt very uncomfortable in that low sitting go-cart with an old Chevy behind him. Wound up all the way in low gear, the gray car made more noise than the go-cart. The gray could go maybe thirty—two to thirty-five miles per hour in first gear and Willee didn't bother to shift.

After about three laps, Mike was far enough ahead to pull under the shade tree and be safely out of Willee's way.

Willee stopped, still in the parking lot and not chasing Mike under the shade tree.

Mike stood up, looked directly at der Nerd, and said: "You're crazy!"

Willee grinned big. "Yes, I am, aren't I?"

Mike grimaced. "When I get a car it will be faster than yours."

Connecting Rod Cornflake

Willee took the old gray mare west on highway I-70 to Columbia, Missouri. It was June in a college town so school was just ending. Turning around there, der Nerd started making his way back toward Saint Louis. Willee passed big rig trucks with his left elbow out the window, a couple fingers on the steering wheel, a Camel in his right hand, and looking more for the ashtray than the highway.

Eventually, a blue Corvair four-door with four college students, most likely going home for the summer, passed him. Der Nerd pulled out the dashboard throttle and followed that car nearly a hundred miles. He left his right foot stretched across the front seat since he had that dashboard pullout.

Somewhere west of St. Charles he pulled into a gas station. The gauge told him the car needed gas but he knew it also needed oil. It wouldn't have done much good to check since there wasn't enough oil to reach the dipstick.

He had only two dollars in his pocket so he had to choose. To him, the logical choice was to buy gas. Better to get back home with a busted engine than to have an engine full of oil in a car that couldn't get him home.

On his way home, a connecting rod started knocking. The knocking was getting worse and Willee noticed he was almost to the exit he'd take to go to Jimmy's house in west Saint Louis County. At least it would be a place to stop and think.

When he got to Jimmy's house he saw the result of his handy work with that mailbox.

"Jimmy, I need a ride home." The rod was knocking bad by this point.

They decided to leave the busted gray car in the parking lot of a nearby Methodist church. Jimmy knew his parents wouldn't want it sitting outside their house. Willee was glad it wasn't a Catholic church since he was Catholic. He didn't want to bother the priests about having such a sinful car. Besides, if they'd known him they probably would've charged him storage.

Jimmy gave Willee a ride home. Lenny was at work, but Willee's Uncle Gene was visiting. Willee told Gene what happened. Gene got a tow truck to take the car to the dealership and then drove Willee there.

It cost about half as much to fix the connecting rod as the whole car had cost just a few months earlier.

Be assured Willee will return to further damage the gray Chevrolet.

Stop This Thing

Willee was helping a buddy, Rich, cut grass for extra money during the summer of 1962.

After they finished mowing, Willee went to stow the hot lawnmower in the trunk while Rich went to get paid. Willee had to pick the lawnmower up to get it in that trunk. His arms were a bit tired but he'd never admit it.

Upon leaving, he drove to Brown Road and made a right turn heading toward Saint Charles Rock Road. Trying to beat oncoming traffic, der Nerd accelerated as fast as that old six would go.

Well, the driver's door must not have latched when Willee got in the car earlier. Without a seatbelt on, he fell partway out of the door. His head was low enough to see under the open door.

"Stop This Thing!"

Rich had the radio turned up pretty loud and hadn't noticed that anything had happened. Willee, meanwhile, was staring up at an oncoming yellow and black 1956 Mercury. Rich was oblivious.

The Chevy kept turning right, maybe to avoid the newer and bigger Mercury. A tree was able to stop the Chevy but also caused Willee to bump his head on the ground. Willee got back into the car quickly so as to avoid embarrassment.

"Woah, you were really lucky. That could have been really bad," Rich said after he understood what happened.

"Yeah, right. I don't get hurt easily."

A couple of weeks later his dad asked how the front fender on that gray Chevy got dented.

"It ran into a tree".

His father never pushed the matter. His father also did not know how lucky Willee was.

Residential MG

There was a day in the summer of 1962 when Willee was obeying the red light where Olive meets North and South Road. An MGA of 1956 vintage pulled up next to him and revved its engine. The race was on. They both revved their engines waiting for the green light.

An MGA is not a drag racing car, it is a sports car meant to take corners. A 1950 Chevrolet is only meant to get you from here to there, not at a particularly high rate of speed.

They both took off when the light turned green. After going about a block straight, the residential street made a ninety-degree bend to the left. While Willee actually beat the light blue MGA across the intersection, the MG took the corner tight. He made it inside okay with Willee hanging outside. Willee knew a turn was coming but for some reason or other did not trust his brakes.

Have you ever wound up at fifty miles per hour in a residential parking lane? It was okay for the MG in the regular street lane - he just had to watch for cars pulling out. Willee neatly missed all the parked cars. It might have caused fear in him if he'd had any sense. It was, though, hazardous to the residents who hadn't left for work yet.

His bald, squealing tires were keeping everyone on the sidewalk, making the way clear for the MG ahead of him. The squealing tires through the residential neighborhood early in the morning were loud enough to wake up any residents who thought they might sleep in.

Willee did not even get into second gear during this first leg of the race. Having determined he'd become his own worst enemy by possibly letting the MG win, der Nerd jammed the old gray mare into second gear and tried to catch the MG on a short straight. He got close as they came to a ninety-degree right. The MG made it fine. Der Nerd tried to brake and double-clutch for a downshift.

Willee did not spin out. He only hurt his own pride. He did learn that he could not do three pedals with only two feet - not without more practice.

Drag Race

Although the MG beat it racing through residential streets of University City, Willee was not about to give up on that gray car. A high school friend, Jim, had a 1949 Ford V8. They agreed that a race between a '49 Ford V8 and a '50 Chevy six might be interesting.

They chose an empty parking lot as that would be an easy way to get enough space. The Schnucks grocery store on Olive near 82nd worked well since grocery stores were not open on Sundays back then. It was a drag race but nowhere near a quarter-mile. It didn't really matter to them as they both were relatively new to driving.

Willee got into second gear before realizing that Jim had stalled the Ford V8 coming off the line. Fortunately, Willee's brakes were working at that point and he was able to stop before going into the bushes. Jim didn't need brakes. Willee counted this as a win, but not one he'd brag about.

Springdale

On a warm Saturday in the summer of 1962, Jimmy stopped by Willee's house. He'd been in the area to run an errand for his parents and decided to hang out for a bit. When Jimmy arrived, Willee and his date were about to head over to Rich's house in Overland. Rich and his girlfriend wanted to go to Springdale and talked Willee into driving them. Jimmy accepted Willee's offer to go with them.

Springdale is a swimming pool and playground on highway 141, just east of Fenton, Missouri. It was new back in 1962.

They had a nice time but had to leave after a while. On the way out, Willee's date asked to swap seats with Jimmy, who had sat in the back on the way there. She liked Willee well enough, but she was nervous about the shaky steering wheel. It would shake every time they went over the slightest bump on Lindbergh.

Willee could calm the shaky steering by scrubbing the tires against the curb. At sixty miles per hour it took a little accuracy or a lot of blind luck to scrub those tires. He closed his eyes every time he got close to the curb. That was to avoid noticing the vehicles that were desperately trying to avoid him.

A couple of days later, Willee took the car to a small garage recommended by his father to get the steering fixed. The old man didn't want the dealership mechanics to see how destructive Willee was with that old gray Chevrolet.

The problem was the idler arm. It is supposed to be held on by three nuts. It was now held on by only one, which was loose. At this point, he realised luck, or nerdluck as he would call it later, works both ways. He was starting to see the dangers of not taking care of his car.

Back in the Races

Having won his first drag race, Willee went out looking for competition on the streets. The first one he found took place at the corner of Pennsylvania Avenue and the Rock Road, which was paved by 1962. It was against two Chrysler Imperials. Those cars had 413 CID engines and each had a load of kids inside.

The truth of the matter is they were going east on the Rock Road which becomes Easton as you enter Wellston.

Willee knew the old gray mare could get across the intersection pretty quick. Those big cars took a little time to accelerate. Willee was in the slow lane. Entering Wellston, the four-lane road became two lanes due to parking. The in-town speed limit was thirty miles per hour. The big cars couldn't continue to accelerate due to a slower car in front of them. All Willee had to do was move into the remaining traffic lane ahead of the other cars, in which case he declared himself the winner.

That is how the old gray mare with a stock 216 engine beat *two* 413 CID Chryslers. This is a win he would brag about.

Spinning Mud

When Willee first got the old gray mare, it had reasonable tires for a $125, twelve-year-old car. The tires did not remain reasonable after racing go-carts, Corvairs, MG's, Chrysler Imperials, and Flathead Fords.

Willee didn't pay much attention to the tires as long as they remained inflated and sort of round. He did have a tire pressure gauge which he used to check them for between thirty-two and thirty-five pounds. Anywhere in that range was okay according to what he'd read, although he had some trouble understanding the logic. It didn't seem that air weighed anything so why did it weigh something in tires?

Anyway, there was, at one time, a rear tire that refused to remain inflated. To compensate for this, der Nerd inflated that tire to sixty pounds, enough to keep it up overnight. He didn't think the tire ought to sleep while he was awake worrying about it. Going out Olive Street Road he spied a pile of tires in an abandoned barn and thought he might get himself a replacement for his leaking one. There was no driveway, just a muddy field to get to the barn full of old tires.

Willee did not take any of the abandoned tires. Instead, he got stuck in the mud because of the over-inflated bald tire on the old gray mare. It would spin and spin and dig itself deeper in.

With no tread for traction, the tire had no choice. But Willee had a voice and invented a few new words. When the speedometer reached thirty, he banged the car into second gear as the car had not moved an inch. The act of shifting somehow caused the other rear tire to get traction.

An old Chevy six is not going to perform well on the pavement when starting in second gear. However, slithering through the mud with the speedometer reading about forty, der Nerd got it rolling forward at maybe five to ten miles per hour. The problem was the traffic on Olive Street Road was going about fifty. Pedal to the metal, the gray car would do about fifty-five in second gear. Willee thought that was the best way to merge with the eastbound traffic so he floored it. The speedometer went almost immediately to fifty-five miles per hour. The car was still slipping, slithering, sliding, and not making very fast forward progress. The fortunate thing was the drivers on Olive saw this mud-slinging spectacle and slowed down. This was only to keep some distance between themselves and the nut behind the wheel of the now two-toned, mud over gray, Chevy.

He merged okay with the eastbound traffic while the spinning, bald, and mud-coated tires were trying to get up to speed. It is hard to imagine an old Chevy six burning rubber in second gear but might be realistic to think it was spinning mud. Mud painted itself all over the trailing cars.

After getting out of that, Willee decided it was better to just keep inflating the leaky tire for now. He has plenty of excitement without getting stuck in the mud.

Tired Tires

Willee put the spare tire on to replace the flat rear tire so he could bring the flat to a nearby garage. Upon waking up the next morning, he looked out the window and saw the old gray mare had another nearly flat tire. Oh, well – all he could use was the hand pump to put more air in it. Being lazy, he decided just to sit around and watch TV for a while instead.

Sitting there in front of the TV, Willee became visible to his father who needed ice for a house party that evening. There was a City Ice station on Page just east of Hanley Road. Willee took the money from his father for the ice, grabbed the hand air pump from the carport, and went out to the old gray mare.

It was a nerdluck day – there was another flat tire on the other side of the car that couldn't be seen from the house. Willee had to report to his dad that he had two flat tires and could not inflate them and also get the ice back, all in the required time period of fifteen to twenty minutes.

The old man really wanted that ice. "Take my car – here are the keys".

It was not, however, Lenny's car. It was a company car. A white 1962 Chevy four-door hardtop with a two-barrel 283 CID and power everything. Willee was familiar with this car as it was just a later version of the same vehicle he'd first learned on with his uncle Gene.

He cautiously proceeded to the ice house. The ice house worked similar to a vending machine. Willee put the coins in. Then he had to figure out the buttons. There was blocked, cubed, or crushed.

After messing with buttons he didn't understand, Willee finally got a bag of ice and returned to the 1962 Chevrolet. Hurrying to get home and deliver the ice before it melted, he accelerated westbound on Page Avenue. Not racing, just getting to the forty miles per hour speed limit.

The intersection was coming up and Willee covered the brake pedal with his left foot, a habit learned from driving a car with no or low brakes.

He learned a few things after reflecting on how he got into the 360-degree spin.

1. There is very little play in a power brake pedal.
2. When the brakes lock while you are turning the wheel, you can go in an unanticipated direction.
3. When the vehicle comes close to going in the correct direction, take your foot off the brake and floor the gas.
4. Power steering helps a lot.
5. If you can't find the right direction the first time, let the car spin again. Don't worry about the other cars as they are already making strange manoeuvres to avoid you. You just have to avoid getting dizzy.
6. Don't scuff the white sidewalls but do wipe the dust off the bag of ice so the old man will never know what happened.

Lenny never did find out about the close call. Willee brought the ice inside to his dad and then went to his room to read car magazines with his radio on in the background.

Corny Conscience

Back in 1962, there were many farms along Missouri highway 79. The cornfields came to nearly the shoulder of the highway, which was only a two-lane road, but it had a wide shoulder. Willee and a couple of friends went for a drive in the old gray mare. When they got to this area and saw all the corn, they decided they'd like to take some for their families so everybody got out to pick some. In total there were about two dozen ears picked, far more than they needed. They put the stolen corn in the trunk of the car and decided whether to keep going toward Hannibal.

The corn was forgotten about until a few weeks later. By then, der Nerd could not ignore the stench no matter how many windows he opened or how many Camels he smoked. He looked in the trunk and found chunks of brown and black stuff that used to be yellow and green. If he'd only known the secret of adding water and sugar, he could have gone into business for himself making stuff for Junior Johnson to deliver.

Willee now had the problem of disposing of the fermenting corn without letting his parents know about it. There were no big black trash bags like we have today, no way to disguise the smell. The best thing is to return the fermenting corn to the farm along the highway. This will also return the stolen property to its rightful owner, absolving the theft.

This done and engine not destroyed, Willee slept with a clear conscience. The trunk still stunk but odoriferous material had departed.

End of the Line

There were a couple of other incidents before that old '50 gray
Chevrolet gave itself up. After having thrown another rod,
Willee had to get it fixed. The mechanic's name was Shorty.
He often bought cigars at the same little store where Willee
bought candy back in grade school. He also worked on cars for
Willee's uncle and the shop was only a couple of blocks from the
house where Willee lived. Shorty was married and drove a light
blue 1952 Chevy at the time.

"You went eighty-five on those tires? It isn't safe. There's no
tread."

"They are still round. What about the connecting rod?"

"That's fixed. Here's your bill. Just don't drive over fifty
for the next five hundred miles. Let it get broken in instead of
broken again."

Willee tried to take Shorty's advice seriously. He did watch
the speedometer and did not get much over fifty miles per hour.
After a couple of days, der Nerd remembered the old gray mare
could only do fifty-five in second gear.

Shorty did not tell Willee *not* to do the fifty miles per hour in
second gear. He also did not know which end of the horse he was
talking to. Willee just left the car in second and quit watching
the speedometer.

Willee did get more than five hundred miles out of the new connecting rod. But he also managed to get all six rods knocking before junking the old gray mare for fifteen dollars. It takes a real Nerd to throw eight rods in a six-cylinder engine. At least that's what Willee told his uncle many years later.

That 216 CID was splash lubricated, not full pressure. Might run as high as fifteen pounds of oil pressure - not the thirty to forty of a full pressure system.

Willee had driven that car for about ten months before junking it at a yard on the other side of Lucas and Hunt from Normandy High School. It was very relaxing for a sixteen-year-old to open the hood after dark, let the car idle, and watch sparks crawling down the ignition wires. He might have been better off to replace ignition wires than connecting rods. Looking at it logically, replacing ignition wires would have caused the engine to run better and blow more rods.

II

Adventures in Old Gold

That '55 was not a really fast car
but it was particularly brave
What else could have given its guts
To this nerdy knave?

Gold Hub Caps

In November 1962, the gray car went to the junkyard. They got a trade-in at the dealership where Lenny ran the books. It was a gold 1955 Chevy BelAir four-door sedan, two-barrel 1959 V8 engine and Powerglide transmission.

Gold was a factory color in 1955 but there was also a gold Chevrolet paint, Fiftieth Anniversary Gold, offered in 1962. This '55 had the 1962 paint but it was nosed and decked, had a 1954 Corvette grille, dual exhausts, and 1957 Oldsmobile spinner wheel covers. Not exactly stock but nobody considered a four-door sedan a real hot rod.

Willee was out to prove them wrong. The first thing he managed to do was lose one of those Oldsmobile wheel covers. By the time Willee slowed down enough to turn around, somebody in a blue and white 1955 Olds was on the side of the road picking up that wheel cover.

He chased the Olds but didn't catch it. It might have had something to do with the fact that the five-and-a-half foot short guy, Willee, did not want to personally confront the heavy six-foot guy. It might also have had something to do with the fact that a two-barrel 283 CID engine could not keep up with a 324 CID four-barrel Olds regardless of how much the driver weighed.

Lenny did not like the fact that the *new* used car was already missing a wheel cover and he got his son four 1958 Chevy standard hub caps. The three remaining Starfire wheel covers went into the trunk of that gold '55, which was okay until the cops found them.

Follow That Car

Willee and a high school friend named Gene were cruising University City residential streets. They spotted two girls turning off Delmar in a green and white 1956 Chevy convertible. Willee couldn't decide whether he was more interested in meeting the girls or racing the car. Either way, he attempted to follow it and got stopped by the cops.

In the trunk, they found the three Oldsmobile Starfire spinner wheel covers, some tools, and some miscellaneous parts. They assumed these had been stolen.

"Where did you get these wheel covers?"

"They came with the car."

"There are only three."

"I know. One fell off and got picked up by a guy in a blue and white Oldsmobile."

They then noticed the yard sign advertising "Leonard Kennon for Alderman".

"Who is Leonard Kennon?"

"My dad. He's the one that bought the standard Chevy wheel covers after I lost the other Oldsmobile one."

"Why do you have his sign in your trunk?"

"He got elected and told me to get it off the lawn. A trunk is a perfect place to put junk."

"So your father is an Alderman?"

"Well, he got elected. Personally, I just consider him an older man."

The second cop went to the other side of the car to try and hide his laughter. It embarrassed the first cop who was stuck with Willee by himself.

They didn't even give Willee a warning! The cops drove away first so Willee left a patch of rubber following them. Luckily for Willee, that '55 was not a fast car.

Gaining Confidence While Losing

Early in his drivership of that 1955 Chevy, Willee raced Jim in his 1962 Olds. The Olds was the family car, a stock two-barrel 394 CID but had ten and a quarter compression.

Jim and his brother had already raced it at Alton dragstrip. It was pretty quick for a full-sized Olds sedan and didn't even have a four-barrel carb. They won a trophy sticker at Alton but couldn't put it on the Olds because it was the car their dad drove to his Boy Scout meetings, all over the midwest.

Anyway, der Nerd wanted to see how his *new* '55 would perform against an almost really new 1962 Oldsmobile so they staged a race on Pennsylvania Avenue from Page to the Rock Road. At that time, there was a cemetery at the Rock Road and a Chuck-A-Burger at Page where Willee worked as a carhop.

Despite Willee's efforts, the Olds won, doing about eighty-five when it had to brake for the intersection. Willee made it to seventy miles per hour in Powerglide Low. This is pretty good for a two-barrel hydraulic lifter engine - close to seven thousand RPM. The RPM is based on Willee's later calculations coming from a published 1959 PG Corvette road test - he did not have a tachometer.

He only lost by about five car lengths. This early race gave Willee some confidence in that gold '55.

Altar Boys Burning Rubber

This story has a place in the early part of Willee's drivership of that gold '55.

At Saint Rita's Catholic grade school, boys were drafted to serve as altar boys at morning Mass. Two boys were drafted for each mass and a schedule was hung up on the bulletin board at the school which was on North and South Road, almost two blocks north of Page. Rich was often Willee's partner in the altar boy assignments.

Not long after Willee got the gold '55, he stopped at a Clark gas station on Olive just west of 82nd Street early in 1963. Rich was running the pumps at the time. Rich filled up the car and Willee paid the twenty-one cents per gallon for full service.

"Neat car, Willee. Will it burn rubber?"

"I don't think so, it's a Powerglide."

That planted the thought in der Nerd's head but he didn't know that Rich had just washed down the gas station lot prior to closing for the night. It was a very slippery surface since oil floats on top of water. Willee experienced it that night. He sort of slid sideways around the gas pumps and aimed the car for Olive Street Road. There was no oncoming westbound traffic and der Nerd knew the car would do seventy in low gear. Pedal to the metal and transmission still in low, the tires were slipping in the watery oil. The speedometer registered over fifty when that vehicle made it to dry pavement, possibly at fifteen miles per hour.

Willee aimed for the westbound lane. Old Gold got sideways again but somehow pointed west. Had there been any traffic that night, der Nerd would have merged sideways when he hit the dry pavement. It is an absitively posolutely unique experience to go sideways in a two-lane driveway. No one could have entered the station with Willee leaving sideways. Then he hit dry pavement going in the right direction at approximately sixty on the speedometer. This is with no forward progress since the car was going sideways at the time.

Forward did become forward when he hit the dry pavement. That car left between thirty and forty feet of rubber and oil on Olive Street Road. Willee had to go around the block to come back and measure it as best he could, just shy of two car lengths.

So the '55 survived Willee again even though Willee's driving might have been a sin.

Another Flathead Ford

Lots of kids back in 1962 liked flathead Fords because they were the cheapest way to get modifiable V8 transportation. In fact, Fords had been in that category for years.

On a rainy day early in 1963 and early in the days of Willee's drivership of that gold '55 Chevy, he came up to the stoplight at Woodson and Page. Next to him was a blue and white 1951 Ford driven by the older brother of one of his grade school classmates. The Ford was a two-door hardtop much neater looking than a four-door Chevy. And der Nerd was familiar with an identical appearing 1951 Ford being built by a high school acquaintance. That one was powered by a J2 Olds engine which had three deuces - factory equipped but not by Ford.

Not knowing how this Ford hardtop was powered, der Nerd decided he had to race it when the light turned green. Besides that, he sort of somewhat remembered the driver of the Ford from grade school and believed it would be a fair race.

They were going east on Page from Woodson. Because the street was slick, der Nerd attempted, against his natural tendencies, to accelerate somewhat slowly. When the cars got to the top of the hill on Page, at what was then Town and Country mall, in spite of letting the car run sort of normally he was somewhat ahead of the Ford.

The other guy got a ticket for running a bald tire on the wet street. Willee just cruised on, pretty sure that the Ford he had just raced was not powered by an Oldsmobile V8.

Several months later, the brothers owned a white 1956 BelAir four-door hardtop. Why would a couple of kids trade a Ford two-door for a Chevy four-door? Because it was faster!

Der Nerd was disappointed he never got an opportunity to race against that 1956 Chevy.

Snow Drift

Willee did take several kids to school in that gold '55. He also drove them home. Sometimes on the way home, he would pick up Gene's girlfriend from nearby Mercy High School. They picked her up once during a hailstorm so she wouldn't have to wait for the bus in that weather.

They did it another time during a snow storm. Traffic wasn't moving on the roads so der Nerd thought her bus would be late. Since traffic was not moving on the roads, Willee decided to take a shortcut across Heman Park, a fairly large municipal park in University City. The gold car did manage to avoid the swimming pool. Willee wasn't against letting it swim, but only in warmer weather. You wouldn't normally think of a '55 Chevy being involved in water sports back in 1963.

After bumping over railroad ties that surrounded the parking lots, he simply drove through the snow-covered softball fields and left the park directly in front of Mercy where Val was waiting for her bus.

Well, it wasn't exactly a simple ride. Everybody had to sit in the back seat so the car could get traction in eight inches of snow. It had to get up enough speed to get over the railroad ties bordering the parking lots. Once on the softball fields, the car was going maybe thirty miles per hour. The speedometer read higher because the rear tires were spinning. It did go sideways in various directions but got across the street okay. That's only because drivers on the road stopped, not understanding what this car was doing. Exiting a snow-covered softball field sideways is not exactly normal.

Streetcar Tracks

Willee had an idea to try out and got some friends to go with him. It was early 1963. Old, unused streetcar tracks ran next to Delmar Boulevard, between Pennsylvania Avenue and Hanley Road.

The group were on a residential street just north of Delmar with the streetcar tracks running between. The residential street had a slight curve near the dead-end which was heading toward the streetcar tracks. The dead-end had a chain-link fence at the end so drivers wouldn't try to take a short-cut across the tracks to Delmar.

This particular ride was occurring at night, but Willee had noticed a large hole in the fence during daylight hours. Someone had apparently tried to take the shortcut in spite of the fence. Since the streetlights were along Delmar, not along the tracks, and there were none on the short dead-end, der Nerd decided the cops wouldn't notice him if he doused his own lights. It was Willee's nutty thought to see if he could fit through the hole in the fence without damaging his own car.

That '55 got through the fence okay but could not cross the tracks at that point so he turned right to go west and follow them. Actually, the left wheels were bumping along the track ties while the right side of the car attacked overgrowth along the unused streetcar right-of-way. Der Nerd made an attempt to keep up with the traffic on Delmar but passengers complained at thirty miles per hour about bumping over the railroad ties. They didn't like the fact that he wouldn't use his headlights either, but he intended to remain invisible to the police.

Traveling slower now at the passengers' request, Willee noticed the bumps from the railroad ties suddenly stopped so he did too. On the right was another dead-end street that was part of the residential area. Access to the dead-end was blocked not only by a chain-link fence but by a metal barrier that stretched completely across the roadway. It had once been a through-street to Delmar.

The street was old blacktop that had turned gray with age and was overgrown with weeds, but at least it was a real street. If the car could get through the weeds, they could do thirty instead of the current five to ten. He backed up a little and moving forward again made a hard right.

"Willee, this is a real street. The cops can't give you a ticket for being on the tracks. You could turn on your headlights now," said a nervous passenger.

"If they see me, they'll wonder how we got here and give me a ticket for putting a hole in that fence."

"At least the drivers on Delmar will see you coming," someone else said.

"You can't even see this street from Delmar it's so overgrown! They will be more distracted wondering where we're coming from."

Having gotten used to going slow due to the railroad ties and complaints, Willee sort of snuck up on Delmar Boulevard. The '55 hugged the left side of the gray blacktop, then swung sharply to the right as it neared Delmar. Willee was sure both rear wheels were on pavement and he was angled correctly to merge with westbound Delmar traffic. Semi-hidden behind the overgrown streetside weeds and positioned ready to merge, at approximately a forty-five-degree angle, der Nerd waited for a gap in the traffic. When he saw a gap coming, he simply floored that gold '55 and aimed at the tail lights of the last car on Delmar. There was twenty feet of gray blacktop to get initial traction on pavement. Had Willee been positioned correctly, the gap in the traffic was big enough for a normal, slow and cautious, ninty-degree right-hand turn. But he hadn't anticipated anything normal and wasn't prepared for a routine situation so he did it abnormally.

"You're on the street now, turn on your lights," said one of the more cautious kids.

"Slow down, you're gonna hit that car!" This exclamation came from a guy who was currently taking driver's training in high school.

"What car?" Willee asked loudly. "I can't see nothin' cuz weed leaves got on the windshield and I can't see through 'em."

"Turn on your windshield wipers."

"It ain't rainin' and I ain't got no squirter," Willee replied.

"Turn on your headlights."

"I only got two hands," der Nerd replied. The left was on the steering wheel and the right hand on the radio dial.

Der stupid driver could see the taillights ahead, even through the leaves, when he took the time to look. He saw the brake lights come on and hit his own brakes. He stopped without hitting the car in front. They were at a stoplight and someone got out to remove the weeds from the windshield. At a full stop, Willee removed his hand from the steering wheel and turned on the headlights.

The rest of the night the gold car stuck to solid pavement and didn't disobey traffic rules. At least not enough to risk a ticket.

Field Trip

Willee's school got a day off school in spring of 1963 for a teacher's conference. He and some friends had planned a trip to Hannibal, the former home of Mark Twain. Willee's girlfriend, Donna, did not have the day off as she attended a private school. However, she was getting good grades and decided to skip school so she could go on this trip. She did not bother to tell her parents.

Donna sat next to Willee in the front, as a girlfriend would do. The three guys rode in the back. They had the radio blastin' but der Nerd was trying his best to observe the posted speed limits, even when he had to slow down to read the signs.

That '55 hadn't gotten far out of St. Louis County, they'd just turned onto highway 79, when they got pulled over. The cop suspected them of being truants and of stealing the car. Willee explained that University City High was closed for a teacher's conference. The cop checked the license and registration then went back to his own car. He radioed his dispatcher to contact the school district to make sure there was no school that day at U–City High.

Several minutes later the cop returned to that gold '55 and asked each of the passengers if they attended University City High. Everyone said yes, including Donna, and he let them resume their journey.

They entered the town of Hannibal and stopped for lunch at a hamburger joint. It was by far the greasiest hamburger Willee had ever eaten. Nobody got sick, though. They did a little sightseeing but quickly had to begin the return trip because Donna had to get home at her normal time since her parents didn't know she'd skipped school.

The ride back to Saint Louis was most interesting and not too easy on that gold '55. The Beach Boys tune Fun, Fun, Fun was high on the charts. Every time that tune came on the radio, der Nerd sunk his right foot a little closer to the floor. He was trying to avoid keeping the beat on the gas pedal, which would not have been good for the car.

When the Beach Boys came on the radio that '55 would get going ninety to ninety-five on county roads. The first time, they sort of took to the air when cresting a hill.

Donna said, "You'd better slow down."

Der Nerd did back his foot off the gas but knew the car would be harder to control without the additional force of acceleration. They went from one side of the road to the other on the downside of the hill until Willee stepped on the accelerator again. If you press on the accelerator even slightly going downhill the car goes even faster. If you step on it hard enough to regain control the car will damn near bottom out at the foot of the downhill. When they got to the bottom of the hill, there was some noise from the tailpipes scraping the road. The car kept going and nothing fell off.

The tune ended. Willee got reasonably close to what he thought might be the speed limit. Donna calmed down, but because she had practically screamed when the car tried to fly, the other passengers were nervous.

However, the DJs were not through playing that song. It came on every twenty minutes or so and Willee's foot always had the same reaction. In order to avoid jolting the already nervous passengers by letting that Powerglide drop into passing gear, he kept the speed over seventy. That increased when the tune came on and after a couple more times, Donna would lean over and watch the speedometer when the record started to play.

"You're going to fast," became a repetitive reminder every time the speedometer needle passed eighty.

When they got to solid pavement, the steering was just as bad as it had been on the bumpy roads. This worried Willee enough that he voluntarily slowed down to the speed limit. It was a good thing they got to paved roads when they did.

Everybody got home safe but the steering was getting pretty loose. Turns out it was a lower-left ball joint. That would be the one that took all the abuse from the railroad ties along the streetcar tracks.

Go-Cart Rematch

One day when Willee noticed he was low on gas, he chose a station at Hanley and Page. After paying, Willee took a drag off his cigarette while walking back to his car. He happened to see an old friend, Mike, gassing up there as well. They'd had a race in a park about a year and a half earlier. By now, Mike had changed his go-cart out for a black and white 1956 Holiday Hardtop Oldsmobile.

"That's a really neat car. Wish my dad could have got me one like that." Mike said.

Now, why would a kid with a recently acquired 1956 Olds two-door hardtop, 324 CID engine say that about a 1955 Chevy four-door sedan?

Mike was no longer worried what Willee would do if they raced, seeing as he was higher up from the ground. They decided to race going west on Page Avenue and put their pedals to the metal. They had to stop for a red light at North and South Road, another cross street. They both took off when the light turned green. A few cars behind them was a cop that neither had seen.

Both boys raced away. The cop had to weave through traffic. Willee saw the fuzz lights and turned right on 82nd since he was in the right-hand lane. Mike was a couple of car lengths ahead so Willee later congratulated him on winning that race. The cop followed Mike west on Page. Mike got past the Vinita Park city limit sign and the cop quit chasing him.

Neither got a ticket since a single cop can't go in two directions at once. A lesson Willee learned is if you're going fast enough, you can get out of the cop's jurisdiction before he can get your licence number.

Animal Distractions

It was a foggy, drizzly night in spring of 1963. Der Nerd was with his friends Rich and Gene heading north on Lindbergh just driving around. They turned where Lindbergh and Old Saint Charles Road meet and began a southbound return trip.

Der Nerd was still accelerating, sort of sideways into the passing lane on Lindbergh when Rich, riding shotgun, saw an animal on the side of the road.

"Look, guys. What is that?"

Willee turned to look and see if he'd know. They were still going sideways at fifty-five miles per hour in a forty-five zone on a slick road.

At that point, the driver's side windshield wiper blade dislodged itself and flew to the curb a couple hundred feet in front of the animal.

To avoid scratching the windshield with the metal wiper wand, der Nerd pulled over to the side of the road, southbound on North Lindbergh, and put a tire valve cover on the end of wand arm.

They drove back home with this half-inch thingy acting as the windshield wiper for the driver. Rich quit looking for animals by the side of the road. He was very well occupied trying to tell Willee which way to turn the steering wheel. It wasn't until much later that Willee would realize this was a skill he could improve at.

Sore Ear

After the trip to Hannibal, rides on two-lane roads going north became routine. What they called cruisin' at that time, to Willee, meant going from hamburger stand to hamburger stand looking for races.

Of course, when you pulled into the drive-in restaurant, you were supposed to order something. Willee found himself spending more on food than on gasoline. The interior of that gold '55 got coated from more than one malt, possibly due to passengers trying to drink them while der Nerd was driving erratically.

He found a solution - a little hamburger joint in Moscow Mills. It was a drive-in with curb service. There was always a 1955 Ford in the corner of the parking lot but it must have belonged to an employee because it was never occupied. That '55 Ford was the real lure but the curb service girls were cute, too. Sometimes there were even two of them. The burgers were good, as well.

In addition to driving something like sixty miles for a soda and burger, trips to Moscow Mills gave the car a lot of exercise, which Willee badly needed. Der Nerd couldn't do the required number of laps during gym class but managed to pass with a D. He would have done better if the gym teacher had let him use the car.

Going out to Moscow Mills eliminated the street races around Saint Louis where the Powerglide '55 usually lost. Although it was possible to pass on Highway 61, there weren't many races on that two-lane road.

The trips to Moscow Mills provided entertainment on Friday or Saturday nights for several months until Willee wound up working two jobs in the summer of 1963. There were lots of races, but never against that '55 Ford.

One day Willee and Rich made the trip. On the way there, der Nerd had heard a noise that made him worried he had a bad universal joint.

When they were about to head back home, Willee asked Rich to sit in the back seat and listen for it. Rich spent most of the way home on all fours on the floor of the backseat with his ear on the floorboard hump. He found it hard to keep his balance due to Willee's erratic driving and got a sore ear from bouncing off the carpeted floorboard.

Willee wasn't sure that a bad u-joint in a rear-wheel-drive car even makes noise. Rich was basically listening for the drive shaft thumping against the floorboard. It was Willee's intent that Rich give him advance notice that the driveshaft was coming loose so he could slow down. He didn't want to be powering through a curve and lose a drive shaft sixty miles from home.

The driveshaft didn't come loose. Rich wasn't happy about his ear but Willee had convinced him it was worth it.

A Bath and a Convertible

Some friends, of both genders, who rode with Willee to high school seemed to be embarrassed by the dirty car in the spring of 1963. It was actually covered with salt residue from winter topped with dust and pollen from spring breezes.

The friends decided to give the car a bath. This took place in the driveway of Donna's house. It couldn't take place where it lived as Willee would only let his old man see him wash the gold car on Christmas day in 1963, several months after this episode.

They began washing it and sort of thought der Nerd might lend a hand since it really was his car. After some goading, Willee began polishing the chrome exhaust tips. The others finished the entire vehicle while der Nerd waxed the outside and cleaned the inside of those twin exhaust tips.

Earlier in the spring, Willee found out a high school acquaintance was building a 1953 Ford convertible. It was powered by a Flathead engine with two two-barrel carbs.

At that time, Willee did not much care for that gold Chevy. He wanted to ask the kid if he would trade cars, knowing there wasn't much chance.

Now that his car was clean, he thought he should at least try. "For that gold car? No way!"

He'd have to live with this car for a while longer.

Of course, Willee did not have the title to the '55 so he couldn't have traded it anyway. Although his dad bought it from the dealership where he worked, the title was in his mom's name, even though she did *not* have a drivers license. However, to register the car, the Missouri Department of Motor Vehicles document says the registrant "cannot have drivers license suspended or revoked". Well, if she hasn't got a license, it can't be suspended or revoked, can it?

To Bowl or Not to Bowl

In the spring of 1963, Willee and some friends would sometimes go to Tropicana Bowling Lanes on Clayton Road, in the city of Clayton. Der Nerd only occasionally bowled. He wasn't very good at it, but it was better than golf.

Willee wanted to save his money for gasoline instead of renting bowling shoes so he became the designated scorekeeper. He would sit at the scoring table and fall asleep by the second or third frame. Yes, he could fall asleep in a crowded thirty-two lane bowling alley on a Friday night.

The rest of the group got disgusted at having to move him in order to keep their own score. He got tired of being woke up just to move a couple of inches. The end result was Willee would just take them to Tropicana, go for a ride, and come back to pick them up. That ride was out highway 40 to where it met I-70, then east to Brown Road.

There was a place on 40 known as Gumbo Flats where it became a three-lane highway. The middle lane was for passing in either direction but you had to make sure the passing lane wasn't already in use by an oncoming vehicle. Willee learned a few handy things on that stretch of road.

First, if you put your foot to the floor in a Powerglide car, it is likely to go into passing gear. Second, passing gear is a good thing to use if you want to accelerate quickly to get around slower vehicles, which you should do with a shared passing lane. When you're in that middle lane, you are a target for oncoming vehicles so you don't want to stay out there too long. Third, farm trucks use that center lane when they want to turn left. Forth, farm trucks that do not have taillights are hard to see from the rear after dark and you can't see them from a far distance if your own headlights are on low beam. Keeping your headlights on low beam is the proper thing to do out of respect for other drivers. Fifth, when you take your foot off the gas to step on the brake, the transmission comes out of low, passing, gear and goes into drive, eliminating all of the engine braking assist. Sixth, when you lock all four wheels with the brakes, all four tires squealing make a lot more noise than two tires trying to accelerate. Four locked wheels make the vehicle harder to control but the noise alerts other drivers to use caution around you.

Drivers in the right lane slowed down to let Willee in so he could avoid the farm truck. Or maybe they slowed down to avoid being hit by an out of control Chevy. There was no accident, but it was not Willee's fault that there wasn't.

Jack vs Gas Tank

Several friends were with Willee on this day in the spring of 1963. They were cruising along the Rock Road when a tire went flat. Der Nerd noticed this from behind the wheel and pulled into a parking lot. He removed the spare tire and jack from the trunk with help and encouragement from his friends.

Der Nerd proceeded appropriately by loosening the lug nuts while the tire was still on the ground, then jacking up the car. It was a rear tire so he jacked it up by the rear bumper. There were a few unfortunate circumstances.

The '55 was on a slight incline heading uphill. The Powerglide was in Park but that only locked the transmission, not the differential.

Fortunately, the spare tire was inflated. After jacking up the car sufficiently to install the spare tire, Willee removed the loose lug nuts and pulled the flat tire off. Pulling the wheel away from the brake drum jerked the car a little, causing it to roll backwards, down the hill. The car rolled over the jack stand which got stuck beneath the gas tank and forced it edgewise into the asphalt parking lot. The good thing about this was it stopped the rearward progress of the car. The bad thing was the jack was now underneath the car and there was no way to retrieve it or to elevate the vehicle to mount the inflated tire.

A resourceful passenger suggested they go across St. Charles Rock Road to a gas station and borrow a floor jack. Upon arriving and explaining the situation, the attendants looked across the street at the strange position of that gold car in the parking lot.

To Willee's surprise, the attendants let the kids borrow a jack with a very small deposit. The jack was on wheels and they had to escort it across four lanes of traffic to get to the parking lot.

The inflated tire installed and the bumper jack recovered, several of them put the hydraulic jack in the trunk of that '55 and drove across the Rock Road to return it to the service station. The jack was so big the trunk would not close. Didn't bother Willee, though – he was looking out the windshield.

Full Stop

Willee was supposed to pick up his father at the airport. It was drizzling when he headed out. Der Nerd pulled up to a stop sign on Brown Road and sort of accidentally came to a full stop. The engine had quit running. Der Nerd started a process of slow thinking rather than panic reacting. He kept slow thinking while cranking up the starter motor and running down the battery.

Eventually, der Nerd determined that there was no gas. The gas gauge registered about a quarter of a tank because of the dent from the incident a few weeks earlier with the flat tire and the jack. His theory was the dent would not allow the float to reach the bottom of the tank and allow the gauge to proclaim it empty.

A mile walk to a friend's house produced only an empty gas can. Another kid down the street had a new, red 1963 Falcon convertible. He took der Nerd to a filling station to put some gas in the can. Returning to Old Gold after the gas had stunk up the interior of the new Falcon, Willee put the gas in the tank. The engine barely turned over because of the nearly dead battery but it did eventually start. The friend with the red Falcon convertible took himself and the gas can home. Der nerd proceeded to the airport.

The old man was standing by the curb, luggage beside him,

cold and wet.

"What took you so long? I've been waiting here for two hours."

"I ran out of gas."

"That's why you have a gas gauge."

"Yeah, but it don't work. It still registered a quarter tank when I ran out."

Willee did not impart any further information. His father insisted they stop at the nearest gas station and fill the car's tank.

The 1955 Chevy came with a sixteen-gallon fuel tank. This time it took almost fifteen gallons to fill it. Willee figured that since the tank was dented its capacity was diminished and that they were running just slightly above the level of fumes when they stopped for gas.

Der Nerd's smartest moves of the night were turning down the radio, rolling up his window, using headlights and windshield wipers, and not telling his dad the story about the gas tank and the jack.

A Strange Set of Coincidences

This particular incident occurred in early summer 1963. That gold '55 was still a Powerglide car. Proceeding east on Page from Woodson, Willee accelerated heartily. The hill on Page crested at the Metal Goods plant parking lot entrance and descended rapidly approaching Walton Road. There was a stoplight at the Walton Road intersection at the bottom of the hill.

Der Nerd was travelling at sixty to seventy miles per hour on Page, a forty miles per hour zone. The light turned red as he descended the hill. Brakes alone would not stop the '55 in time, even though they did function on this occasion. He downshifted that Powerglide into low thinking if it could accelerate to that speed, it could decelerate from that speed. The '55 did stop at the white line. Unfortunately, it really stopped. The engine would not start. After the light turned green and traffic cleared, Willee pushed the gold car catty-corner across the intersection to a service station.

Willee found two mechanics on duty. They pushed the gold car into a service bay to work on it. In the other bay was a red 1956 Cadillac.

The problem with der Nerd's '55 Chevy was that the cam had jumped time.

"What did you do?" asked one of the mechanics. According

to his shirt, his name was Larry.

"I was going a little fast and had to stop for a red light so I downshifted into low."

"You shouldn't do that with a cold engine," Larry said. "Thick oil and cold metal can cause the rotating parts of an engine to become misaligned."

"You outta just buy a Cadillac," the other mechanic, Gene, said. "It will accelerate just as quick but does it on torque, not RPMs."

"Yeah," said Larry, still under the hood. "And Cadillacs have bigger brakes. You won't have to downshift and over-rev a cold engine."

Gene said, "We both own Cadillacs. That's mine in the next bay. His is the yellow one on the lot."

Both were 1956 Caddy two-door hardtops, two-tone cars with white on top.

They got the gold car running and Willee went into the office to pay.

He asked Larry, "Do you really think your heavy Cadillac can beat this Chevy on acceleration?"

"Of course it will. We're changing shifts and I'll be leaving soon so we can find out for sure. I'll be going east on Page. You can leave first. I'll follow you out of here and beat you to the top of the hill," he replied.

Willee turned back to the office desk to sign the receipt so he could pay the bill and get his car. The mechanic behind the desk had signed his name at the bottom of the bill signifying the work was complete. His last name was McAnulty.

Staring at the man behind the desk, Willee asked, "Do you know a Benny McAnulty?"

He's our brother," was the almost simultaneous reply from

both mechanics. "You know him?"

"Yeah, I go to high school with him. Last year I would drive him to FINA stations where he pumped gas but he's got his own car now."

"Not much of a car," one of the brothers said.

"But he wouldn't have an old Chevy," said the other brother. "Benny told us this kid he went to school with managed to throw eight rods in a Chevy six."

"No, I only had two rods fixed but all six were knockin' when I junked it."

"That was you?"

"Yup. And you think I can't beat you to the top of the hill?"

"We'll find out as soon as you pay your bill. Just don't hit anybody."

"Oh, I never hit people or other cars."

The Caddy did win, but Willee would stick with Chevy for a while.

About twenty years later, der Nerd attended his sister-in-law's wedding. She married Gene McAnulty. Benny was there, too. He and Willee talked for a while at the reception. He was dressed in a fine suit and had a beautiful wife. A totally different person than the high school kid that old gray Chevrolet took to those FINA stations. Willee wore a grumpy looking business suit and was with his wife who was not particularly happy with her sister. She was not unhappy with the marriage, just didn't like her sister.

The Stop Sign

Another incident around the summer of 1963 on McKibbon involved Willee and a friend, John. Although they were only seventeen years old, they had gotten into a little bourbon at John's house. Maybe John got into more than a little. Willee was cautious of the thirty miles per hour speed limit and was observing it. John simply opened the passenger door and stepped out while they were moving at thirty miles per hour. He only got a few bruises from it. Later he explained, "I thought we were at a stop sign".

They would become casual drinking buddies during their final year of high school. When Willee joined the army he still had a half-drunk bottle of vodka in his bedroom desk. It was most likely finished off by his mom after she found it while cleaning one day.

Years later, Willee would see how bad it can go when a person gets behind the wheel of a car after they've been drinking. He would vow to never again do that.

Racing on the Streets

It was the summer of 1963 and the gold car still had a two-speed Powerglide automatic. Going east on the Rock Road, Willee stopped for a red light at Carson Road. Another '55 Chevy pulled up in the left-hand lane next to him. There were two guys in the front seat of the two-door hardtop. It was a stick shift and the driver gunned the engine waiting for the green light. Having learned this from his uncle, Willee simply looked at the other driver and nodded. The race would be on when the light turned green.

Willee knew nothing about power breaking with an automatic and simply put the pedal to the metal when it was time. The stick shift hardtop burned a little rubber and beat Willee's car over the crest of the hill. But der Nerd had gotten smarter and shifted into Drive at about sixty on the downhill side. He almost caught the stick shift hardtop by the next light and the cars were side-by-side again waiting for the green.

The guy riding shotgun in the hardtop yelled over, "What you got in that thing?"

"Two barrel 283 Powerglide," der Nerd replied. "What you got?"

"Four barrel 265 with a Corvette cam. Wanna try again?"

"You betcha."

They had three stoplight to stoplight races that night and the hardtop won two of them but did not actually *run away* from the gold sedan. Willee was proud of his car.

Construction Zone

Willee and his car spent a lot of time travelling on I-70 in 1963. Portions of the highway west of Saint Louis were still under construction.

In this particular spot, MODOT was building an exit ramp. There were orange construction cones blocking access to the right-hand lane and there was a speed limit sign noting the temporarily reduced limit because of the road work. Seeing as it was lunchtime, the blocked lane was empty of workers and their vehicles. Willee decided to get in some driving practice.

The posted speed limit was forty miles per hour so he slowed down to eighty. He then began to weave in and out of the orange cones. Knowing the best way to keep a weaving car under control was to accelerate, he did that and exited the construction zone at something over a hundred miles per hour. That car managed to avoid the big striped sign that stated "end of construction" and managed to miss all of those orange cones. The dumb nut behind the wheel did manage to lose the highway a couple of times but the '55 was able to avoid damage.

Competing with stationary construction cones at eighty to one hundred miles per hour can be hard on tires, though.

Willee's old man was still the bookmaker at the Chevy dealership across from the Fisher Body and Corvette plant. A buyer of a brand new '63 Chevrolet did not like the standard tires and was going to take his new car to a tire store in East Saint Louis. Somehow Lenny heard about this and decided to appropriate those tires for his dumb son.

The standard tires were black walls so Lenny had them installed on new wheels with white portawalls.

The '55 was originally equipped with fifteen-inch wheels but the new ones were fourteen-inch. Der Nerd switched to the fourteen-inch wheels. He kept the old fifteen-inch ones but did get rid of bald fifteen-inch spare. He had to - the extra four tires barely fit in the trunk along with the spare parts and other junk he put in there.

Muffler Holes

Willee had driven up and down McKibbon Avenue in Saint John a few times on a morning in the summer of 1963. He was aware of the cop car parked on the side of the road and was sure it was a speed trap. The speed limit was thirty so he didn't go over that when passing the police.

Eventually, the cops just got tired seeing that sort of hotrod-looking four-door sedan, or maybe they just wanted to get Willee off the streets of St. John. The cops pulled him over and gave him a ticket for illegal exhaust noise.

It had taken him a long time to get those mufflers to sound good. You run the car up to seventy or eighty miles per hour, shut off the ignition, and floor it. This loads the mufflers with raw gas and when you refire the engine the gas tries to explode. Do this often enough and you can acquire holes in the muffler.

Both of Willee's had to be replaced so that car could pass inspection at the Saint John police department, which turned that ticket into a non-moving violation and cost very little.

Willee was disappointed, to say the least. He considered starting over with the new mufflers. Maybe somewhere far away from Saint John. Someplace out in the middle of nowhere would be ideal.

Jaguar DQ

Der Nerd almost kept up with an XK-120 Jaguar in a street race. Unfortunately, that race took place in front of the Dairy Queen where Willee worked. Der Nerd was officially on break and considered it a real piece of luck to find such hot competition in a short span of time.

The DQ owner saw the race and informed Willee that the highly identifiable gold four-door sort of hot rod would not be allowed in the DQ parking lot if it ever raced in front of the store again. The customers would get a bad impression of the employees.

Willee complied. Though not completely out of respect for authority. He never again found a race that appealing.

At Least He Didn't Set the House on Fire

It was a Sunday afternoon and der Nerd took a little ride. The purpose of that ride was to determine the cause of a noise coming from the back of the car. If the '55 had louder mufflers, he never would have heard the noise.

The ride became longer as he tried to determine the source – he even turned down the radio in order to hear the noise better. Eventually, he determined it was a rear-wheel bearing so he drove home and told his dad.

The ol' man got discounts at the Chevvy dealership where he worked. The plan was for the ol' man to go there and open the service bay door, then bring Willee home when the car was locked inside the dealership. Then Lenny, the ol' man, would turn in the service order when he went to work Monday morning.

The ol' man took his own route into the city limits. It was the route he took regularly to work but one der Nerd was not familiar with. From the Rock Road, Willee turned left on Carson to get to Natural Bridge. There he would turn right and head for the city and the dealership. About halfway to Natural Bridge, der Nerd noticed a Corvette pulling out of a subdivision behind him.

Ever anticipating a race, der Nerd kept an eye on the Vette

behind him. It was an earlier model, not a Sting Ray. It had single headlights, meaning a '56 or '57, but it was red and white with side sculpting. As der Nerd watched out of his rearview mirror, he noticed a constant cloud of smoke billowing out behind the Corvette. Willee thought that if the Vette had a really sick engine, he might have a real chance against it. After all, der Nerd almost kept up with an XK-120 Jaguar.

There was a slight downhill as Carson Road approached Natural Bridge and a stop sign at the bottom. There were also stop signs on Natural Bridge. Saint Louis did have a lot of stop signs. Willee took his foot off the gas and signalled for a right-hand turn, hoping the smoking Corvette would follow. Natural Bridge was a four-lane road and the two cars could race side-by-side.

As Willee went to make his turn he stepped on the brake pedal lightly but it went to the floor! Der Nerd could drive that old gray '50 with no brakes but this came as quite a surprise to him in the '55. His first inclination was to double-clutch, downshift into first, and shut off the ignition. A simple three-step process he had frequently used in the old gray mare. This time, it wouldn't work. A Powerglide equipped car has no clutch. If Willee pulled the column shift lever toward himself and down, as if to reach first gear in a stick shift, Powerglide would have gone into reverse.

Willee decided it would not be a good idea to shift the transmission into reverse at twenty to twenty-five miles per hour. Instead, he reached for the emergency brake. In a 1955, the emergency brake is to the left of the steering wheel. Willee reacted as he did in the 1950 model where the emergency brake was on the right. He reached down with his right hand and grabbed the under-dash gauges. This did not slow the car at all.

Being about twenty or thirty feet from the intersection at Natural Bridge Road, where the lane he was in would end, der Nerd decided he'd better turn. He had signalled to make a right and the blinker was still on, he thought it best to go that way. Besides that, he would at least be attempting to turn in the same direction as the cars he was going to hit, since they expected him to stop and would probably maintain their right-of-way.

Der Nerd cranked the wheel and stepped on the gas to keep the car upright going around the corner. The other drivers avoided him, which was a wise move on their part. He rubbed the tires against the curb to slow down while searching for the emergency brake.

The car stopped in front of a house on Natural Bridge and der Nerd exited the gold '55. He noticed an orange glow and a lot of smoke from a rear brake drum, which is very close to the fuel tank. Running up to the house, Willee knocked on the door.

"Can I borrow your phone to call the fire department? My car's burning."

They invited the grubby kid in, looked up the number for him, and let him use the phone.

After making the call, Willee waited outside for the fire truck. Several members of the family had gathered on the front porch to watch the action.

The fire truck arrived. They squirted the brake drum to cool it off and keep it from igniting the gasoline. When the orange glow left and the smoke departed, a fireman asked where der Nerd had been going.

To Jantzen Chevrolet to get the wheel bearing fixed."

"Are you going to drive it there?"

"Can't - it's an automatic."

The fireman gave him a puzzled look and said: "This smoldering brake drum didn't hurt your transmission."

"I know that, but it ain't got no brakes. I could do it with a stick shift but I don't know how to stop an automatic with no brakes."

The fireman walked away with a confused look on his face.

Willee had the car towed to the dealership and his ol' man drove him home. They missed Ponderosa, the TV show, but der Nerd considered himself fortunate that he did not get a ticket for running the stop sign and that all the other vehicles managed to evade him.

Another Loss

Dale was a friend in the same County Tech data processing class as der Nerd. His family car was a dark blue Olds station wagon.

Willee was driving to high school with a carload of kids. This was one of those rainy days when Willee decided not to use his windshield wipers. Although that '55 had electric wipers, der Nerd thought if you can learn to drive without brakes, you can learn to drive without windshield wipers. That was poor logic on his part since he couldn't drive the Powerglide with no brakes.

Willee was turning right onto Olive. Dale honked and waved as he went by in that Olds wagon. He was on Olive, not speeding, and also had a carload of kids in his car. The gold '55 was easily identifiable to all the passengers in Dale's car.

Willee accelerated hard trying to catch that Oldsmobile but he was starting from a dead stop. He was tired of getting beat by Oldsmobiles. It was a ninety-degree right turn and the car slipped on the wet pavement and sort of got a little sideways. Of course, that made all the passengers lean or slide in the direction of the skid which made it get more sideways.

Willee understood that turning on the windshield wipers would not help rear-wheel traction so he didn't bother. He just peered through the rain covered windshield at the Old's taillights and followed it to school. This loss made him more determined to win a race against an Oldsmobile. He'd take any opportunity he got.

Foggy Night

It was a foggy night in spring and Willee decided he could use some practice driving in stuff he couldn't see through. One friend decided to go along 'cause he wanted to share a story about his girlfriend. The fog wasn't bad in University City and they started up Lindbergh at a reasonable pace. The fog got worse as they neared Lambert Airport. Why does fog seem to home in on airports?

With visibility down to two or three car lengths, Willee reduced his speed slightly and turned off his headlights.

"Why did you turn out the headlights?"

"They create a lot of glare. I did leave the fog lights on."

"You don't have fog lights."

"No, they're called parking lights according to the owner's manual. But we're not parking, we're driving in fog."

"How can you see anything without the headlights?" the friend asked.

"I couldn't see anything with them except the fog. What difference does it make?"

"Maybe you ought to slow down a little."

"I already did. I'm only going thirty now and that's the speed limit."

"I can't even see the road!" said the friend.

"Well, that makes two of us."

"How do you know you're even on it?"

"Because the ride is smooth, just like pavement."

"Slow down! There are tail lights ahead."

"Don't worry, it's a Cadillac with some rich guy driving. He won't even notice we passed him," said Willee.

"You're going to pass him?"

"I will not stop behind him. But you can tell we're going in the right direction 'cause we could see his tail lights."

"Why is he stopped? Maybe there's an accident up there."

"He's probably looking for the road he spent so many tax dollars to prepare."

"You're making me very nervous. What if he opens the door?"

"I'll just put the pedal to the floor. He'll never know what hit him."

Nobody got out of the Cadillac and no one got hurt. Willee did turn the headlights on when they reached I-70. He determined that he'd had enough practice with fog, at least for a while.

Catch That Hubcap

Dale, whose father owned a hardware store had recently gotten a 1957 Ford. The '57 was replacing a 1952 Ford four-door automatic six that Dale had acquired from his aunt.

Dale was driving a bunch of kids home from school in his green and white 1957 Ford two-door hardtop. As he was leaving the parking lot, he drove by the gold '55. One of the passengers held up a hubcap to the back window of that '57 Ford so der Nerd could see it. Willee thought it looked familiar so he immediately checked his and saw he was missing one. Passengers were still piling into that '55.

"Hurry up and get the doors closed," Willee yelled. "They took my hubcap and I'm gonna get it back!"

Dale didn't realize any of this was going on and drove normally. He stayed near the speed limit through a couple of residential blocks and stopped to make a proper left turn onto Midland Boulevard. It is west of Heman park and about two blocks east of U-City high. Willee was in hot pursuit at some multiple of the posted speed limit but didn't have time time to look at the signs. Anyway, he left the Powerglide car in low gear in case he had to slow down suddenly. Besides, leaving it in low made the transmission act as a governor so der Nerd would be limited to seventy miles per hour, which he considered fast enough for residential streets.

Willee backed off the gas closing in on that '57 Ford as it was beginning the turn onto the main road. The way he figured it, since Dale had actually come to a full stop and looked for traffic, there wasn't any.

It was a wide ninety-degree left turn Willee took at only thirty miles per hour. Dale was just gradually accelerating and correctly took the left lane of the four-lane road. Willee made a wider turn and was in the right-hand lane.

The '55 rocked to the right while making that turn. That threw the passenger weight to the right. Some of the kids screamed, some fell on the floor, and some multitasked.

Something alerted Dale that he was being pursued by the nutty Nerd. It could have been the kid who stole the hubcap not wanting to get caught. It also could have been the squealing tires or the screaming kids in the '55. Another possibility is that Dale saw the sideways Chevrolet and didn't want his new used '57 Ford nailed by it. Whatever it was, he floored that Ford and sped away.

Willee kept the pedal to the metal, too. His current mission was to keep at least a couple of the four wheels on the ground. He managed that, as well as stopping at the next red light. The Ford was already gone. Der Nerd made the determination that an engine can only produce so much power and if you use it going sideways rather than forwards, you don't get there as fast.

The next day went better. Dale returned the hubcap polished and with an apology that he didn't know the other kid had taken it. It was, after all, just a 1958 hubcap, not a wheel cover. Its value was about two dollars. No one had suffered any physical injury.

Willee would later teach three of those screaming passengers how to drive – in the '55!

Snow Plow

Tim was another friend from the same County Tech data processing class as Willee and Dale. Tim had a metallic green 1955 Chevy 210 CID two-door sedan and brought other students from Ballwin who were involved in sheet metalworking. Tim's Chevy was a six and he really couldn't race it with all those passengers.

On a snowy winter day, Dale had car trouble and needed a ride to school. On the way to County Tech, the weight of all those passengers wouldn't let Tim get up a hill in the fresh snow. This occurred where Lucas and Hunt Road meets I-70.

Since Tim couldn't make it up the hill to the overpass and entrance ramp, he decided to take a shortcut to the highway. He spun the wheel and started down the unpaved slope which separated the access road from the highway. This would have been grass-covered ground in summer but on this winter day was covered with deep, freshly fallen snow.

Tim could not get much acceleration when he started down his shortcut to the interstate because the car had to plow through about six inches of snow. While the weight of five or six passengers did not help with the traction, that weight did help with the eventual acceleration. It had a lot to do with gravity and inertia and maybe E=MC squared, at least that was Tim's explanation. So he aimed for a break in traffic and a relatively smooth route across the drainage ditch to the highway.

Unfortunately, because he had gotten some momentum, it was going across the snow without really digging in. Tim applied the brakes and turned the steering wheel, aiming for a vacant spot in the slow-moving highway traffic. At that time the green Chevy was nothing but a big roller skate on ice. It spun a couple of 360s and landed on its side in the drainage ditch. Nobody got seriously injured. The cops somehow got everybody to County Tech and Tim didn't even get a ticket for it!

Willee was glad to take Tim and all his riders back to Ballwin, partly to be helpful and partly to show off that **his** '55 Chevy did not wind up in a drainage ditch.

A Load of Passengers

The sheet metal class got out about fifteen minutes later than the data processing class so Tim stayed in the building to direct his passengers to the '55 Chevy that would take them back to Ballwin. Dale and Willee sat in the old car and smoked cigarettes while the engine warmed up.

Dale said he had a motorcycle license but it required him to wear glasses.

"You don't need them to drive a car?"

"No, that license is unrestricted. But the motorcycle thing is a problem."

"Why?"

"The helmet don't fit over the glasses."

They were going southbound on Lindbergh to take the group back to Ballwin. Around Page, der Nerd's uncle rolls up to the gold car in the passing lane. Uncle Gene was driving that blue and white '59 Chevy that Willee learned how to drive in. Uncle Gene didn't have any problem racing, although a 1959 four-door hardtop with a two-barrel 283 wasn't exactly the quickest thing around.

Anyway, Gene looked at der Nerd who simply nodded in response. It was how his uncle taught him to accept a race. Pedals went to the floor and Gene began to pull away. Gene beat

Willee, fair and square.

Later Uncle Gene remarked, "I thought your car was supposed to be faster than mine."

It wasn't until years later when telling this story to his daughter that Willee realized the '55 was carrying seven hundred pounds in passenger weight and probably made that thirty-three hundred pound '55 weigh more than the thirty-eight hundred pound four-door hardtop with no passengers.

Willee dropped off Tim and his passengers before heading back to drop off Dale and then going home.

Nut Behind the Wheel

One evening some cops found a door open at the dealership where Lenny worked. He drafted Willee to drive him to the dealer so he could ensure nothing had been stolen. That had to be done so the police could complete their report.

Willee waited in the car there on Natural Bridge Road, right near the still open office door where the cop car was parked. Two young guys, probably in their early twenties, came out of the Chevy plant and walked across the street to the gold '55. They addressed the kid behind the wheel.

One of those burly dudes asked, "Where did you get this car?"

"From this dealership," der Nerd replied, pointing down the sidewalk between the police car and the open office door. That was, by the way, the general direction of the used car lot.

"We were just wondering," The other guy said. "It was built by a friend of ours named Tom Woods."

"Well, my dad works here and this car was traded in on a Chevy II station wagon."

"Okay. We just wanted to make sure it wasn't stolen."

Those guys turned around and went back to the Chevy plant. Willee lit a cigarette and contemplated. The car still bore a city sticker from Black Jack, a rural community not far from where he sometimes took his sister to horseback riding lessons. But there was something about that name – Tom Woods.

Der Nerd had gone to grade school with a kid named Tommy Woods. While in grade school, Tommy got in trouble for stealing a Caterpillar bulldozer from a construction site. Not knowing how to stop it, Tommy simply parked that big cat in the side of a building.

Nothing had been stolen from the dealership but it was a very interesting short time for der Nerd.

Voltage Regulator

The voltage regulator was a minor incident that took place in front of the family home. For some reason, Willee thought he could get the battery to charge quicker if he shared the voltage regulator.

Several wires under the hood went up in smoke and Willee rushed in the house to call the fire department. A big red fire truck arrived but there was no real fire, although a couple of them had extinguishers in hand.

After looking under the hood, they wanted to be sure the greasy-haired kid wasn't trying to steal the car. Der Nerd showed them the pink registration receipt which he kept in his wallet with his driver's license because the cops usually wanted to see both. The '55 was registered to his mom, who just happened to walk out of the house to see why there was a big red fire truck out front. Or perhaps she just wanted to learn what her kid had done now.

The fireman lectured both of them. "It costs seventy-five dollars to bring this truck and crew out. So don't call us again unless it's a real fire". Willee took that lesson to heart.

This incident was the main reason the old man got Willee the job at Carl's Sinclair station in an effort to teach der Nerd what not to do with cars.

Fuel Pump

While working at Carl's Sinclair station, der Nerd changed over that Powerglide to a stick shift. To install the floor shift, he had to drill holes in the floor pan.

Sometime later, the fuel pump went out. The problem might have partly been caused by the fact that the three-speed had a 2.94 first gear while the Powerglide had a 1.82 low. That 2.94 first gear allowed the two-barrel 283 to turn more than seven thousand RPM, probably because of less air resistance.

Willee called his dad at the dealership to get a new one delivered to Carl's. Carl could get a forty percent discount from a parts house and would have passed it on. By letting his old man pay, Willee was getting a hundred percent discount.

The fuel pump delivered by the dealership to the service station was still in a sealed box and had a part number and a description of the application. The application was "1956 265 V8, 2x4 bbl". Der Nerd was happy to have a fuel pump actually designed to do seven thousand RPM and went about installing it.

The '55 started fine. Willee shut it off to finish his shift. It was nearly dark when he left the service station. He turned left on Wydown and prepared to make a right on Hanley, only a block away. Suddenly he noticed a yellowish-orange glow through the holes in the floorboard. After pulling over to the side of the road, der Nerd got out and opened the hood. The engine was engulfed in flames! Oddly, there was enough fuel getting to the carburetor to keep the engine running.

Willee ran back to the service station to get the fire extinguisher from the office wall. Carl was at his desk in the office and called the fire department. Der Nerd ran to the gold car, really identifiable in the dark because of the flames surrounding the open hood. He went to the front and began spraying at the flames. The proper thing to do is spray the base of the fire, but der Nerd didn't know that and just sprayed at the flames.

A passerby in a suit said, "You have to get closer to put it out."

Der Nerd replied, "I tried, but it's hot in there."

The white Clayton fire truck arrived and the crew handled the situation before the damage went beyond the engine compartment. Willee called his old man to get the '55 towed to the dealership for repairs.

Lenny said, "Be sure to empty the ashtray."

Der Nerd did that as he waited for the tow truck but did not understand why. He understood that was for insurance purposes but he was not smoking around the '55 while changing the fuel pump. He had already been told by Carl that he shouldn't smoke while pumping gas. He was also not smoking at the time of the fire.

There was a carton of Camel cigarettes on the package shelf behind the rear seat. After emptying the ashtray, Willee took the carton of Camels out of the car. It had nothing to do with insurance, he just didn't want the mechanics stealing them while the car was in the shop.

The car came out of the shop a few days later and Willee learned a bit. The two-barrel carburetor was not standard for a

1955 engine or for the 1959 283 under the hood -it was actually a truck carb for a 348 engine. Also, the engine had the Power Pak four-barrel camshaft. It was standard on all four-barrel 283's in 1959 and many other years.

After learning this, der Nerd made an assumption that the car had actually been built to race at Alton Dragway as a stock 265 CID, two-barrel, Powerglide 170 factory rated hoursepower car. It made sense to a seventeen-year-old in 1963.

Easy Win

Jim was riding shotgun in the '55 with Willee one night, going west on Page looking for races. They stopped for a red light at Pennsylvania Avenue. Jim's brother, Larry, was already there in his white 1957 Ford convertible. This was a recently acquired used car, powered by a four-barrel 312 engine.

They took off when the light turned green. The Ford immediately began to pull away from the Chevy. The race got called at around sixty miles per hour. Larry, being a few car lengths in front, saw a cop ahead so his wife didn't want him to go any faster.

Willee was not surprised he lost this race but he was glad Larry saw the cop first and nobody got a ticket.

Camping

Willee joined the army. He was scheduled to leave June twelfth of 1964, the Friday between finals and the graduation ceremony. Since he was going to miss graduation, his friend Jimmy decided that a group should go camping at Johnson's Shut-ins. They chose to go the weekend before Willee's finals since it was his last weekend before leaving. He wasn't worried about studying and most of the kids went to University City High which had finals the following week.

The group took two cars. Willee drove Jimmy, Jim, Gene, and John in his '55. Dale drove the '57 Ford Willee had chased a few months earlier trying to get his hubcap back. He took Tim and a couple of other kids from the County Tech data processing class. They decided to meet Friday evening at Jimmy's house in Ballwin since it was on the way for Willee and most of the data processing group lived out that way.

It was almost seven in the evening when they met and they arrived at the campsite about an hour and a half later. Willee got there a few minutes ahead of Dale. It was dark out, but for some reason Willee wasn't using his bright lights.

"I just need to get the car parked", was Willee's reasoning for not turning his lights on high beam.

Willee didn't hit any trees but he also didn't avoid parking close to them. At least a couple of the guys had to squeeze out of the vehicle.

Dale parked behind Willee and everybody got out. The evening and night went well.

During their first morning, one of the guys noticed Willee's parking job.

"A little close to the edge, huh Willee?" he said while smiling.

Willee's front tires were only a few inches from the edge of a cliff. If he hadn't stopped where he did, he would have driven off it. It was his nerdluck again.

The guys enjoyed their camping trip. When they were getting ready to leave, one of the guys convinced Willee to back the car up before letting the passengers in.

III

In the Army

These stories involve four cars and five engines.

Licensing and Parking

Having junked the gray '50 about twenty-two months earlier, and having been prohibited from taking the gold '55 to Fort Leonard Wood by his parents, Willee wanted another vehicle. It turned out that the first mechanic he had worked for, Carl, was selling a dark green 1950 Chevy wagon that ran on about five and a half cylinders.

Willee bought that car for fifty dollars soon after basic training. His Advanced Individual Training, AIT, was also at Fort Leonard Wood. There were a lot more weekend passes in AIT than in Basic and Willee did put many miles on that car touring highway 50.

The first problem occurred during the first weekend Willee owned that car, but it was not a mechanical problem. It seemed the Highway Patrol thought the vehicle needed license plates. Willee lost the argument and went to Rolla to get the plates.

It basically took all of Saturday because he had never paid property tax before so he had no receipt for the prior year. He had a title for the 1949 engine Carl had installed but the clerk didn't know what to do with it. Willee did also have the title for the 1950 station wagon itself which eventually got processed.

Once or twice the eighteen-year-old Private Willee drove the car home on weekends. Well, not quite all the way home. He parked it about a block from his parents' house in a dinky strip mall on Page Avenue, County Road D. He parked it in front of the store where he bought Rock & Roll sheet music when he was in high school. Then he walked the block to where his parents and sister lived.

He figured if his parents wouldn't let him take the gold car to Leanard Wood, they wouldn't like the idea he had gone out and bought another car to drive there. He was positive his father wouldn't like the idea that the green '50 station wagon was not insured and might try to prevent him from driving it. Also, since his father knew Carl, Willee didn't want to get Carl in trouble for having sold him the car. So he tried to keep that car a secret.

Disposed

The weekend before his AIT group was to ship out to their permanent locations, Willee had to get back to Saint Louis. He had a date on Saturday night. It was with the girl who had been dating his best friend and they were in the process of breaking up.

A couple of guys wanted to fly home before departing overseas so Willee was taking them to the St. Louis Airport. He was also taking another guy, Gary, to his small hometown in southern Illinois. It would be an interesting journey.

It was after dark when they arrived at Lambert Airport. The two passengers departed the vehicle to catch their planes. The generator quit working about that time. Willee drove the wagon to a gas station at Page and Hanley where he had done business for a couple of years. He had the gas tank filled and borrowed an oil can to lubricate the generator. Why der Nerd thought oiling the generator would make it work no one will ever know. Before they crossed the river to the Land of Lincoln, the headlights were brighter and the ammeter needle went from DIS to CHG. Or maybe it was –30 to +30.

They pulled up at Gary's house about 3 a.m. and Gary invited Willee in to rest. Everybody was sleeping but Gary said his mother would fix them a good breakfast in the morning.

About seven in the morning, Gary's mother appeared at the bedroom door.

"What is that station wagon doing in our driveway?"

Gary pointed. "It's his. This is Willee. He brought me home from Leonard Wood for the weekend. I told him he could stay for breakfast."

Willee's eyes were barely open. She looked at him as if asking herself what planet he had come from. What bothered her most was him being on the clean sheets with oil-covered blue jeans and dirty shoes. She did fix a grand breakfast and the still mostly asleep oil-covered mess stuffed himself.

He then went out to the station wagon to begin his way back to St. Louis. The car started, which Willee assumed to be a good sign because that meant the generator actually did charge the battery. A station wagon with a 92 HP 216 engine is not going to be very quick, especially when it's only running on five and a half cylinders. Willee stopped for gas but left the cold engine running, still not sure the generator was working or the battery was charged. To keep the car from rolling, Willee set the emergency brake.

With the car fully gassed and Willee stuffed from a big country breakfast he hit the road again. He was following a light blue stake-bodied truck which he assumed to be a farm vehicle. A later interview proved this to be true. The farmer was not speeding and that kept Willee under control since the five-and-a-half cylinder station wagon could not accelerate fast enough to pass on that two-lane road. He was content to remain about a hundred yards behind the truck until the truck stopped to make a left-hand turn.

Willee would have been content to remain three hundred feet behind the truck and slow down gradually until the guy could turn, but the truck didn't turn. So Willee stepped on the brake pedal which immediately went all the way to the floor. Remembering his other brakeless experience in the 1950 Chevy, he reached for the emergency brake handle. It was already fully extended!

It took der Nerd a few seconds to recall what he had done. He'd left the emergency brake on when he'd left the gas station. While thinking about the cause, Willee failed to think about the solution which would have been downshifting and shutting off the ignition.

The green station wagon introduced itself to the blue truck with a loud BANG. A lot of steam came out of the '50, now having a busted radiator, and the farmer said his stake bed was now a half-inch shorter.

No one was hurt, no charges were filed. Willee was soon to depart for Germany and had not determined how to dispose of the green wagon. He simply took the license plate off, put it in his duffel bag, and walked the couple of miles to the Greyhound Bus Terminal. In his mind, the car was disposed of.

Willee joined the Army to get more data processing experience. His AIT, however, was in administration. That meant running a manual typewriter. He had taken typing in high school and got a "D". He'd gotten an "A" in data processing at St. Louis County Tech so the Army sent him to school (AIT) to learn something he was already not good at. To further complicate the matter, his best score on the tests to determine a "career path" in the military came in vehicle mechanics. He did have to teach a class in vehicle maintenance after stealing that car.

One-Wheel Traction

After disposing of that green '50 Chevy wagon, der Nerd found his way back to Leonard Wood. The Army provided a plane that took him to the east coast where he boarded a bus to go through New York City to the boat. The boat was an old troop ship that had somehow survived WWII and Korea. It did get him across the Atlantic to Germany. Willee got assigned as company clerk to a medical unit in Frankfurt.

There was some kind of rule about enlisted personnel owning private vehicles which he managed to get around. Since he was basically the clerk for the Company Commander and worked with him on a daily basis, the CO signed off on this transaction.

A long term enlisted guy in the medical battalion had brought his family and their car to Germany at the Army's expense. He was selling his '58 Rambler which was a full-sized station wagon, white in color, with a light blue interior, and overdrive transmission. While stateside, the guy had converted the wagon from a six to a 327 Rambler V8. This guy's wife worked at the hospital and had access to Ether. If you put Ether in a Rambler 327's gas tank, it would go almost as fast as a factory 300 HP Chevy 327. Willee bought the car for two hundred fifty dollars and got with it one small bottle of Ether, a gift from the seller.

Willee used that car to move about three miles to the Third

Armored Division HQ when he did finally transfer to the data processing section out of the medical battalion. By then der Nerd had used all the Ether and learned the overdrive didn't work. One of the problems that occurred was a used rear axle half-shaft. The German mechanic at the PX service center told him it was drive train misalignment.

The guy didn't know that Willee had loaded the fuel tank with Ether and popped the clutch a bunch of times trying to race everything he could, from a VW to a Mercedes. Willee learned that while the German citizens might drive a hundred twenty miles per hour on the autobahn, which had no speed limits at the time, they did not get involved in street races. Der Nerd busted the rear axle shaft racing non-racing opponents. Driving it to the PX service area, somewhere in downtown Frankfurt, with only one-wheel traction was a new experience.

Article 15

With the Rambler running again and both rear wheels getting traction, Willee decided to take care of the car and not destroy the drive train by racing it. Instead, he drove over a curb after taking a barracks acquaintance named Nowell to his girlfriend's apartment on the outskirts of Frankfurt. Nowell was from California but did not drive a car the Beach Boys would write a tune about; he bragged about his stock 1952 Chevy!

Willee left the apartment complex and ran over something on his return to the barracks in downtown Frankfurt. The steering was bearing hard to the right. He couldn't turn the wheel hard enough or quick enough to enter his own casern. His casern was on the left so he went to the one on the right, where the PX Cafe was.

He swung the steering wheel hard to the right and because the PX Cafe was closed there was plenty of parking in front of it. Since Willee could no longer turn the steering wheel, he simply let the car park itself. It took two parking spaces, centered approximately on the yellow line between them.

Der Nerd got out to walk back to his barracks but went around the front of the Rambler to look at the damage. The right front tire was partially flat. It still had air but was practically parallel to the ground on its side. He guessed the top right ball joint had fallen out.

"No wonder it didn't wanna turn left," Willee remarked to himself while leaving the parking lot.

Leaving that casern to cross the street, the MP's at the gate advised Willee he could not leave his car there. "It's occupying two parking spaces," they told him.

"I can't move it right now. Needs an upper ball joint, I think."

They gave him twenty-four hours without a ticket. In that period of time, he sold the Rambler to a friend of the guy who had sold it to him in the first place. The guy bought it because he knew what the car was made of. Willee did get five dollars for it and no Article 15. That's the most they can do for an illegally parked car.

Undisposed

Willee bought his first 1957 Chevy in Germany. This '57 was actually a decent car when he bought it for a hundred twenty-five dollars. It was a model 210 four-door station wagon with a V8 engine and standard transmission. It had come from the factory with a 265 CID engine but now had a 1961 two-barrel 283 engine. Willee decided that if the '55 had been sort of a hot rod, then so could this '57. To do that would require exhaust noise. He ran it hard over dusty farm roads until a rock finally punched a hole in the muffler.

After getting it registered, one of the first ventures was to drive several co-workers to a nice restaurant on the outskirts of Frankfurt. They had on Armed Forces Radio Network during the drive and one of the guys really liked "Monday, Monday".

Driving the adequately noisy car through the streets of downtown Frankfurt, der Nerd came upon an intersection where traffic was directed by a cop, not a traffic light. Willee made a left turn and noticed the cop giving him a dirty look probably because of the muffler noise. Not wanting to get a ticket, Willee floored it and sped away before the cop could get his license plate number.

Der Nerd bought a light blue and white 1956 BelAir four-door with a Powerglide transmission and a recently rebuilt 265 V8.

The guy who sold the car was rotating back to the states and didn't want to take the car with him because it was rusty. He sold it to Willee for forty dollars. The problem of having two vehicles was resolved in the next few weeks.

No matter how hard he tried, Willee could not make that '57 perform like his old '55. Rather than burning rubber, he got it to start burning significant quantities of oil. The car still ran okay but not only attracted attention because of the noise but now also because of the trail of oil smoke extending behind it.

Willee thought that since the '57 was burning so much oil it probably needed new spark plugs. He stupidly bought the plugs at the PX. He then borrowed a feeler gauge to gap them and a spark wrench to install them. He removed the ignition wires and installed the new spark plugs. The problem occurred connecting the ignition wires – he didn't label them and didn't know which wire was supposed to go to which cylinder. Taking the quickest solution and avoiding all possible logic, der Nerd took his best guess.

The engine would not start. Willee switched a few ignition wires around but it did not help. On the other side of the parking lot was that '56 with that 265 V8 and it was a lot of trouble to register a privately owned vehicle.

Willee decided to switch engines, junk the '56 and keep the already registered '57. This would equip the wagon with a rebuilt 265 engine, original factory displacement. It would be much harder to break a recently rebuilt engine than one that now used a quart of oil every hundred miles or so.

The Transportation Company was located across the street, the same place where the wheel got so lopsided on that Rambler. A guy who worked at Transportation owned a 1959 El Camino. He would assemble a crew and tow the cars to the transport company's work bays. They would swap the engines for Willee for a decent amount of money. Der Nerd only had two jobs. Stay out of the way of the work crew and buy the beer.

It took them twenty-four volts to start the wagon after installing the '56 engine. At the end of the evening, Willee drove the re-powered '57 wagon back across the road to his own barracks.

Years later, Willee realized he'd probably run the battery down trying to start it with crossed up ignition wires.

Indisposed

The speed limit signs all read in kilometers per hour rather than miles per hour and since der Nerd didn't understand kilometers and his speedometer read in miles, Willee simply ignored them. He just figured that if he kept that three-speed tranny in its 2.94 first gear he would probably not be speeding in town. Depending on the traffic and the terrain the car remained in low gear until it reached a cruising speed of twenty-five to thirty miles per hour. Somewhere in that speed range, he would shift to second.

The engine was so tight that it would not go over 4800 RPM during acceleration. It would get to about 500 RPM in neutral with no load so he could double clutch and downshift to first at a higher speed than he could accelerate to in that gear. This was intentional for two reasons. First, high RPM's would get more wear on the tight engine so it would loosen up and start easier. Second, it made a lot more noise with that busted muffler and it might just backfire and make the muffler hole bigger.

The engine was so hard to start it went through a starter solenoid almost on a weekly basis. No matter how much he tried to loosen up that engine, it wouldn't go fast. The brake lights quit working and der Nerd tried to rewire them outside the wiring harness. After that, the station wagon would not start. Willee sold the not running '57 wagon with no working tail lights for five dollars.

Semi-Successful Repair

Walter was a Warrant Officer in the 503rd Admin Company where Willee worked for about two years. Walter had a Rambler as his family car but it was not a little one. It was the same size and about the same year as the one der Nerd owned and destroyed.

This Rambler needed a repair, a valve job, and der Nerd said he would do it. He took Walter's family car down to the motor pool after hours to use a bay for the repairs.

Walter's Rambler was a stock vehicle and still a six. Using the motor pool service bay was probably the only semi-intelligent thing Willee did regarding this particular operation. When the engine cooled off enough, der Nerd began to remove the cylinder head. After removing the first few bolts, a greenish liquid began exiting the engine block. Willee had forgotten to drain the radiator!

With a loose cylinder head, the car would likely not run, so der Nerd drained the coolant all over the service bay floor. From there it was easy to wash down the drain with a nearby hose.

When the cylinder head was removed all the pistons were topped with anti-freeze. One of Willee's friends came to the rescue and got the car running again. The really odd thing about this is that Walter was a character witness for Willee at his Court

Martial in spite of the fact that he had screwed up the family car.

Taking to the Streets of Frankfurt

Garrett had been a friend of Willee's for a while. He had a Four Season's album with "Silence is Golden".

Willee and Garrett were walking back from the EM club around dusk. They spied a black '58 Chevy Impala two-door hardtop in the barracks parking lot.

"I heard the guy that owns it has rotated back to the states," Garrett said.

"So he abandoned it. Let's look it over."

It had a 348 engine, automatic transmission, and decent red and black stock interior. Willee noticed there was no key in the ignition but it was turned to the Off position, not to Lock.

"Maybe we should take it for a test drive," Willee suggested.

"Where do we get a key if the guy already rotated?"

"We don't need one," der Nerd replied sliding behind the wheel.

He started the car and revved the engine. His astounded companion ran to the other side of the car and climbed into the passenger seat. They rolled slowly past the MP's at the barracks gates. Once on the road, der Nerd wondered how good 348 could run. Instead of going to a place where they could let it run fast, like the autobahn where there was no speed limit, der Nerd drove to downtown Frankfurt. He still wanted a street race like he would have found back in Saint Louis.

Frankfurters just didn't street race. Besides, they couldn't expect a VW or Opel to beat a 348 Chevy. Willee decided the '58 Chevy ran okay and they should take it back to the barracks. Garrett wanted to drive it back and der Nerd thought that was only fair since he already had half of the driving time.

Garrett started driving as they were going down a street by a very large statuesque fountain that was actually squirting water. The statue was in the middle of the street. Garrett would have to slow down to make the hard right around it.

"No brakes!" he screams.

Willee looks at the brake pedal which is all the way to the floor and says "Just take a left. You'll either hit the brick wall or we can coast down the side street until this thing stops."

Garrett was already past the side street but he did turn left. Unfortunately, he missed the bricks, too, and the car finally stopped itself after breaking through the big plate glass window of a jewellery store.

Rear tires hung up on the curb with the engine still running. Garrett escaped to the left and ran down the side street. Willee opened the right-hand door and ran into a crowd just leaving a nearby movie theater. They grabbed him and held him until the Frankfurt police arrived.

The good thing is that with all those people around holding Willee near the car, nobody went into the jewellery store to steal something. It wouldn't have been considered breaking in since the car had already done that.

As it turned out, the '58 Chevy had a new owner so Willee and Garrett had to repay him his purchase price. The big reason for the Court Martial was the eleven hundred dollar plate glass window of the jewellery store. With Walter as a character witness, Willee got only a one rank reduction and a fine that would be deducted monthly.

The end result was that Willee made fifty cents per month for his last six months of service. Unfortunately for the Army, Willee was the guy who printed out the payroll vouchers for Third Armored Division so he knew how much he was getting each month before his CO did.

Since you were supposed to salute the dispersing officer and give your name when reporting for pay, Willee just decided not to report for pay. He didn't care for saluting as they told him that he did it wrong anyway. Why bother to stand in line for a couple of hours just to get fifty cents?

Years later Willee's daughter was just sort of puzzled that someone would go 5000 miles across the cold Atlantic Ocean and to a foreign country to steal a 1958 Chevy.

Engine in the Dumpster

After Willee was court-martialed for stealing that '58 Chevy he was not allowed to purchase another vehicle while in the Army in Germany. So he took a discarded VW engine from a guy who was rebuilding a Volkswagon Bug and put it in the supply storage room.

Willee was not authorized to use the storage room but the supply clerk, Bobby, was a friend and allowed him access. Der Nerd did nothing with that flat-four engine except to visit it occasionally. It is probably the reason he got interested in the flat-six Corvair engine. Both were air-cooled.

There was a major inspection coming up and the rusty VW engine had to leave the supply room. Willee escorted it to a big trash dumpster near a parking lot but could not lift it over the six-foot-high walls of the dumpster-on-wheels so he just left it on the asphalt in front of one of the wheels. The wrecking crew would have to move it to tow away the dumpster. The engine did eventually get picked up and taken off of the parking lot.

Hot-Wiring

It turned out that Bobby owned a 1958 Plymouth which was still in the States. It was an ex-Highway Patrol car with a 383 engine. It was fast and the two of them shared many car stories.

Bobby was on duty one Saturday morning in the stock room when a clerk from 7th Army HQ came in and said he'd lost the keys to his military vehicle, an olive drab early 1960s Ford sedan. Well, there was no way the 7th Army was going to give the 3rd Armored Division keys to their vehicles.

"There is no way I can get you a key," Bobby told him.

"But I've gotta get back. And if I go back without the car, they'll give me an Article 15."

"Oh, well I know a guy who just got court-martialed for stealing a '58 Chevy. Maybe he can hot-wire it for you."

Willee had never hot-wired a car before but he sort of understood how to bypass a faulty ignition switch. And having had a few busted starter solenoids, der Nerd had some idea of how to get around that problem. That Olive Drab Ford six was running within a half hour and the guy was on the road again.

Willee left the army on May twelfth of 1967. While he did not have fond memories of his military service, he had many fond memories of the people he got to know and of the cars he enjoyed working with.

Upon his return to St. Louis, he ran into John, who had gone with him to look at the gold '55 before he'd bought it. He was also the one who stepped out of that car at thirty miles per hour on McKibbon. They stopped at an old tavern where Chuck Berry was still playing loud on the jukebox.

"Did you know your sister was driving that gold '55 after you went in the service? I saw it coming down the street but the driver had real long hair. I knew it wasn't you 'cause they would have cut all your hair off in basic training. Besides that, it was only going the speed limit – I knew it couldn't be you!"

The gold car was long gone by June 1967.

Final Thoughts

Willee never had a Toyota but one of his drinking buddies did and called it "the toy car". Oddly enough, Willee was then on his third 1950 Chevy (when that guy had the Toy Car) - this was the mid 70's.

Willee has had six 1957 Chevy's, two 1955 Chevy's and two 1956 Chevy's.

Willee sold his blue '55 in 1982.

RULE OF THUMB FOR LEFT TURNS ONTO MULTI-LANE ROADS: Left is right but right is wrong.

Everyone reading this: have a good day or give it a try. And remember to buckle up.
    I have had much fun writing and it is not a lie.
    Must sleep now & say buh, buh, bye
    To all of you who read this when the sun is in the sky...
    ...Willee

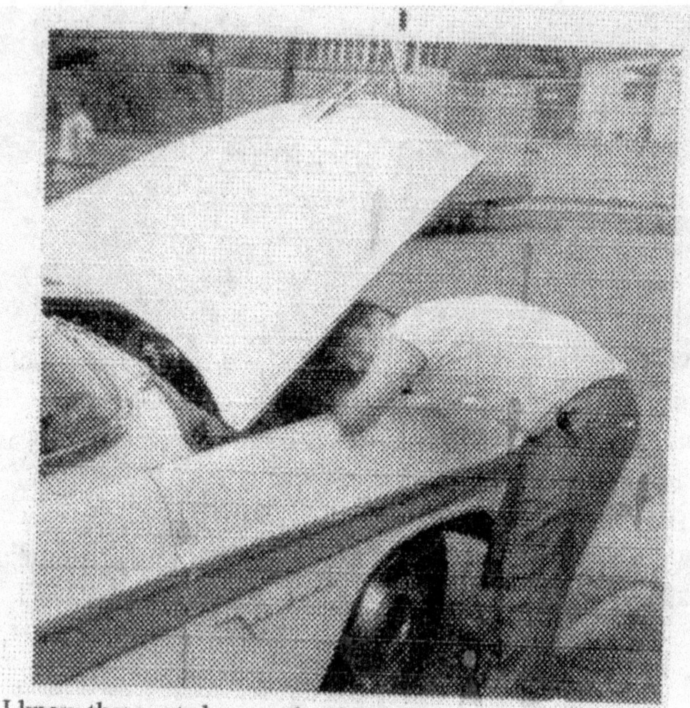

I know there usta be a pushrod in here…

'56 Chevy, taken in '89

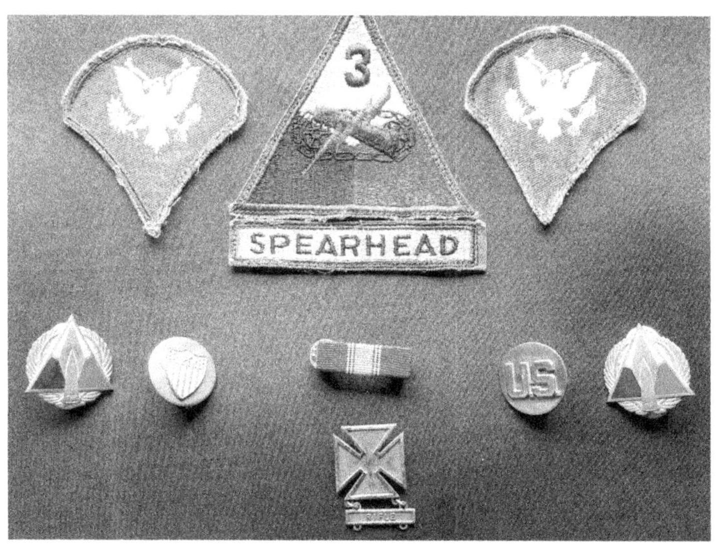